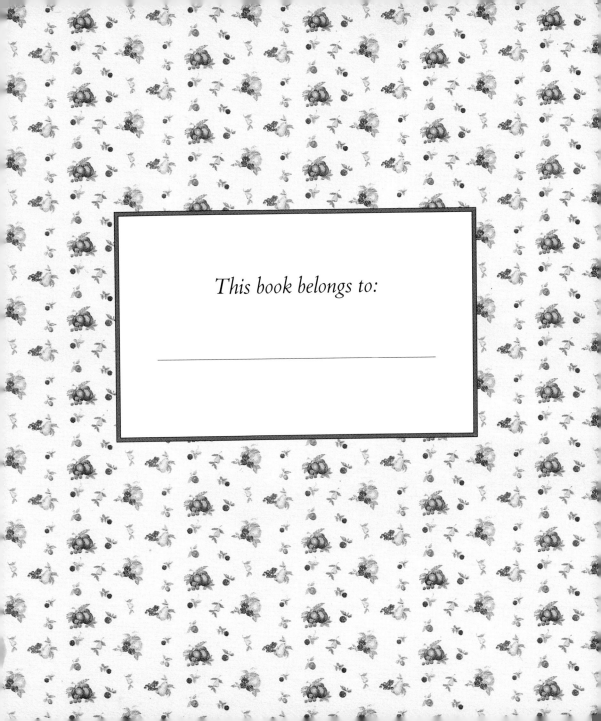

This book belongs to:

_____

Happy New Year, Beni

STORY AND PICTURES BY
JANE BRESKIN ZALBEN

HENRY HOLT AND COMPANY | *New York*

First edition
Published by Henry Holt and Company, Inc.,
115 West 18th Street, New York, New York 10011.
Published simultaneously in Canada by Fitzhenry & Whiteside Ltd.,
91 Granton Drive, Richmond Hill, Ontario L4B 2N5.

Library of Congress Cataloging-in-Publication Data
Zalben, Jane Breskin.
Happy New Year, Beni / story and pictures by Jane Breskin Zalben.
Summary: After constantly fighting with his cousin Max during the
celebration for Rosh Hashanah, Beni discovers that the new year is
an opportunity to put his mistakes behind him and start over.
ISBN 0-8050-1961-8 (alk. paper)
[1. Rosh ha-Shanah—Fiction.   2. Jews—Fiction.   3. Cousins—Fiction.]   I. Title.
PZ7.7254Ham   1993   [E]—dc20   92-25013

Typography by Jane Breskin Zalben
The text of this book was set in Bembo.
The illustrations were done in watercolor and colored pencils.
Printed in the United States of America on acid-free paper. ∞

3   5   7   9   10   8   6   4   2

To Steven, Alexander, and Jonathan—
with love, health, and happiness
for many sweet years to come

When Beni and Sara came home from school, they found a letter waiting for them.

Darlings,
Grandpa and I would like you to come for the
holidays. We've set up the bedrooms. There's
plenty of room. Everyone will be here.
Love and Kisses,
Grandma and Grandpa

"Does 'everyone' also mean cousin Max?" Beni asked.
"Everyone means the whole family," Mama replied.
Beni and Sara groaned. "We're going," Mama said.

So that week, Beni and Sara colored cards for
cousins Rosie, Max, Goldie, Molly, Sam, and
their friends Leo and Blossom down the street.
The morning before Rosh Hashanah, Papa packed up

the car while Mama wrapped the special cakes and
cookies Beni and Sara had baked with their parents
the whole week long. Rugelach. Mandlebrot. Strudel.
Before sundown, they got to Grandma and Grandpa's.

"Beni, darling," shouted Grandma.
"Sara, sweetheart," cried Grandpa.
Then the relatives started coming,
one by one, hugging and kissing each other.

Cousin Max tapped Sara on the shoulder.
He shot a rubber band at her, ran away, and
hid until she lit the candles with Grandma.

Grandpa lifted his wine cup and said the Kiddush. Beni also said the prayer over a round raisin challah. Max started giggling. Beni kicked him under the table. Grandpa ripped the challah. Everyone dipped pieces of sliced apples and challah into honey. "To a sweet, good year! L'shanah Tovah!" Papa cheered. "Let it be a happy and healthy one!"

Grandma passed fresh figs and plump dates around the table. Max stuffed the last dates into his mouth before Beni could eat any. His cheeks were all full and puffed out. Beni made a face. Mama turned to Beni. "Stop it! Save room for dinner," she said. "What did *I* do?" Beni asked, feeling angry inside.

That night, when the cousins were getting ready
for bed, Max put wet plastic spiders and slimy
worms under everyone's pillows. "Now you've gone
and done it! Hippopotamus breath!" Beni screamed.
The parents yelled, "Go to sleep. That's enough!"
Beni wondered, What about a *happy* new year?

The next morning, everyone walked to the synagogue. His grandparents greeted friends when they got inside. Beni picked up the *Maḥzor,* a special prayer book, and read along. Papa blew the shofar like a musical instrument. It made loud, long, sharp sounds. Sara covered her ears, while the little cousins jumped in their seats to see where the noise was coming from.

"What's that?" Cousin Rosie asked, pointing
to the front of the synagogue. Grandpa explained,
"It's a ram's horn announcing the holiday and the
beginning of a new year. Rosh Hashanah
means 'Head of the Year.'"
The rabbi talked about Rosh Hashanah.
"These are the 'Days of Awe.' We look back
at all the things we've done in the past year."
Beni looked at Max. Max stared at Beni,
while the cantor chanted beautiful songs and
the congregation sang.

In the late afternoon, Grandpa asked Beni, Max,
and all the cousins to walk together to a brook.
Many of Grandma and Grandpa's friends were there,
saying prayers and throwing bits of bread into
the water. "What are they doing?" Beni asked.
Grandpa leaned toward Beni. "This is called 'Tashlikh.'"
Grandpa threw a tiny piece of bread into the brook.
"We get rid of what we did during the year that
wasn't so nice and we begin with a new, clean slate.
Would you like a piece?" Beni remembered his mistakes.
He took a small crust of bread from the palm of Grandpa's
hand, tossed it into the brook, and watched it go downstream.

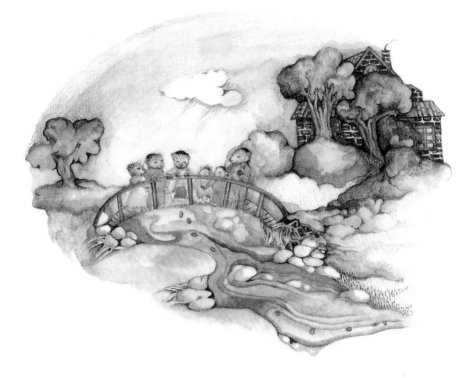

"This is for teasing Sara all the time."
Sara took a piece. "This is for teasing Beni."
Beni took another piece, and gave Max half.
Max ate it and laughed. Beni continued,
"And this is for kicking Max under the
table yesterday." Max bowed his head,
and threw some crumbs into the brook.
"All right, already. I'm sorry, Beni, for
hogging all the dates and figs."
"Me too, Max. I'm also sorry."

Grandpa hugged them both, tightly.
Beni looked up at his grandfather.
"Next year, I'll try to be even better."
Grandpa looked at Beni and whispered,
"Just be you. Happy New Year, Beni."

Max pulled at Grandpa. "I can almost
smell Grandma's noodle pudding."
Beni thought of his grandma's kugel as
they ran across the bridge toward home.
When they got back, Max kissed Beni.

"Yuck!" yelled Beni, wiping the kiss off his cheek.
"Guess I have something to add to next year!" Max cried.
"No you don't!" shouted Beni. And he kissed Max back.
"Yuck!" yelled Max. And they both fell on a bed of leaves,
laughing.

Tante Rose's
Round Raisin Challah

2 packages of dry yeast
pinch of sugar
3 large eggs
1 egg white
1 teaspoon of salt

2 tablespoons vegetable oil
⅔ cup honey
8 cups flour
½ cup raisins
½ tablespoon cinnamon

1. Dissolve yeast in 2 cups warm water around 105°–115°. Add sugar. Stir. Set aside for 10 minutes at room temperature until the liquid foams.
2. Beat 3 eggs and 1 egg white. (Reserve yolk.) Add salt, oil, and honey to this mixture, continuing to beat.
3. Put flour in large bowl. Indent center. Gradually add yeast mixture to flour, stirring center with a wooden spoon until it is absorbed. Stir in liquid from Step 2.
4. Now mix by hand. Fold in raisins and cinnamon. Sprinkle lightly with flour if the dough is sticky. When dough is smooth, place in greased bowl. Cover bowl with dish towel. Keep in warm place for 1–2 hours. Let dough rise until double in size. Punch down.

5. Knead for about 5 minutes on a floured board or surface until the dough tightens and is not sticky. Divide into 3 balls. Form each ball and roll into a snakelike rope about 18″ long. Shape circle by twisting the rope into a spiral with the end at the top of the center.
6. Let it rise again uncovered for 1 hour on greased pan or cookie sheet until doubled in size.
7. Preheat oven to 375°.
8. Brush loaves with mixture of beaten egg yolk and 1 teaspoon cold water to make a glaze on challah.
9. Bake for 20–25 minutes or until golden brown.

Makes 3 loaves.

The *round challah* is traditional on this holiday symbolizing the cycle of life and its seasons. It is also said to be like a ladder to heaven. The bread is more special than the weekly braided Friday-night Shabbat challah for its shape, and it is dipped into honey instead of salt so the new year is sweet and filled with joy.

Glossary

Challah (CHAL-*lah*, with the Scottish *ch* of *loch*): An egg bread traditionally served at a Shabbat meal.

Kiddush (*Kid*-OOSH): The Shabbat blessing, said over a cup of wine.

L'shanah Tovah (*Le-shah*-NA *toe*-VA): A happy new year greeting (literally, "good year").

Mahzor (*Makh*-ZOR): A prayer book used during Rosh Hashanah and Yom Kippur.

Mandelbrot (MAHN-*del*-*braht*): Dry, oblong almond cookies, typically served with tea.

Rosh Hashanah (*Rosh Hah-shah*-NA): Jewish New Year (literally, "head of the year"). Rosh Hashanah and Yom Kippur are called the High Holy Days. Rosh Hashanah marks the beginning of the "Days of Awe" (also called the Ten Days of Penitence), which end on Yom Kippur, the most solemn day of the year. Rosh Hashanah falls in late September or early October.

Rugelach (RUG-*ah*-*lach*): Small, individual pastry filled with raisins, ground nuts, and cinnamon.

Shabbat (SHAH-*bat*): The Jewish sabbath, observed from sundown Friday to sundown Saturday.

Shofar (*Show*-FAR): Ram's horn, blown during the Rosh Hashanah service, to announce the new year.

Tashlikh (*Tash*-LEECH): A ritual where bread crumbs are tossed into a body of water, symbolizing the casting away of wrongdoings to start the new year afresh.